**Customer Service: 1-877-277-9441
or customerservice@pikidsmedia.com**

This publication may not be reproduced in whole or in part by any means whatsoever without written permission from the copyright owners. Permission is never granted for commercial purposes.

Published by Phoenix International Publications, Inc.
8501 West Higgins Road     59 Gloucester Place
Chicago, Illinois 60631      London W1U 8JJ

p i kids and *we make books come alive* are trademarks of Phoenix International Publications, Inc., and are registered in the United States. Look and Find is a trademark of Phoenix International Publications, Inc., and is registered in the United States and Canada.

**www.pikidsmedia.com**

8 7 6 5 4 3 2 1

ISBN: 978-1-5037-5206-1

# WHERE'S DONALD?

Written by Giorgio Salati (Arancia Studio)
Designed by Fabrizio Verrocchi (Arancia Studio)
Illustrated by Gabriele Bagnoli & Beatrice Bovo (Arancia Studio)

*we make books come alive*®
pi kids Phoenix International Publications, Inc.
Chicago • London • New York • Hamburg • Mexico City • Sydney

## DONALD DUCK

Donald Duck is a perfectly ordinary
duck with an extraordinary
personality! Passionate and
emotional, Donald can also
be good-natured and generous.

## HUEY, DEWEY & LOUIE

Huey, Dewey, and Louie are Donald's
nephews and his adventure companions.
They are intelligent, sensible, and brave.
Together, they make a great team!

## DAISY DUCK

Donald's girlfriend, Daisy,
is a remarkable duck.
Dynamic, intelligent, and
full of charm, she loves art
and music. Dancing is one
of her greatest passions.

## SCROOGE McDUCK

Donald's uncle, Scrooge McDuck,
is the richest duck in the world.
He owns endless treasures—
including three cubic hectares
of coins that he keeps in
the Money Bin.

## GRANDMA DUCK

Grandma Duck is the Duck family
matriarch. She is an exceptional
cook, and she tells the most
exciting adventure stories—
most of them about her
own adventures.

## GLADSTONE GANDER

Gladstone is Donald Duck's dapper
cousin. He hates work—which he
considers unsuitable for a duck of class.
But thanks to his luck, he doesn't need
to work to support himself.

## MAGICA DE SPELL

Magica is a sorceress who is directly descended from the ancient Circe. She lives in Naples, Italy. Her ambition is to get hold of Scrooge's Number One Dime.

## DUCK AVENGER

Duck Avenger was born with a mission: to avenge the wrongs suffered by Donald Duck. Now he protects his fellow citizens, too, as the guardian of peace at night!

## THE BEAGLE BOYS

Thieves and robbers (and proud of it), the Beagle Boys are bandits by family tradition, and Scrooge's most formidable adversaries. They carefully avoid any honest work.

## GYRO GEARLOOSE

A practical genius, Gyro Gearloose can assemble one-of-a-kind devices the world has never seen before. This inventor is among Donald's most loyal allies... but sometimes his inventions cause more problems than they solve.

## JOHN D. ROCKERDUCK

For John D. Rockerduck, being super rich is not enough. He wants to be the richest duck in the world! This means he must beat his number-one adversary: Scrooge McDuck.

# LOCATIONS

Look out for Donald Duck and his family and friends as they travel across the globe and beyond! Spot Donald in every location, then turn to the back of the book to see what other characters are waiting to be found.

## DUCKBURG

## UNCLE SCROOGE'S MONEY BIN

## GRANDMA DUCK'S FARM

## DUCK AVENGER'S DEN

## BEAR MOUNTAIN

## VIKINGS WORLD

## A SCOTTISH CASTLE

## QUEEN REGINELLA'S PLANET

## BULLET VALLEY

## DUCKBURG STADIUM

## A MEDIEVAL CITY

## THE BEACH

## GYRO'S WORKSHOP

# DUCKBURG

It's block party time in Donald's neighborhood! The Duck Family is enjoying a day of good food and companionship. Can you spot Donald offering his legendary pancakes to his neighbor? Which one of his friends is aboard a flying scooter?

FESTIV

# UNCLE SCROOGE'S MONEY BIN

Uncle Scrooge's Money Bin needs renovation! But while dozens of workers are busy making repairs, some bad guys are storming the building to steal Scrooge's money. Find Donald and warn him that his uncle needs help!

# GRANDMA DUCK'S FARM

The Peasant Festival is being held at Grandma's place! People from all over the county are here to dance and have fun! Can you spot Donald among the partygoers? Is Grandma Duck dancing or working?

# DUCK AVENGER'S DEN

If you want to hide something, put it in plain sight! Heroes and villains alike are searching for the Duck Avenger, so our beloved superhero has released dozens of his robot clones. Which evil character is conducting his search with a magnifying glass? Now, can *you* spot the real Duck Avenger in the crowd under his secret identity: Donald Duck?

# BEAR MOUNTAIN

At Christmastime, crowds trek up Bear Mountain to enjoy the landscape and the snow, as the area is now a renowned tourist destination! Can you find Donald on his way to cut a fresh Christmas tree? Which one of his relatives seems unhappy to have all these people around?

# VIKINGS WORLD

Donald is searching for a valuable Golden Helmet lost by the Vikings in the Arctic Sea...but a bunch of angry Vikings have come back from the past to stop him! Can you find Donald and help him escape? Can you also spot what everyone is looking for: the Golden Helmet?

# A SCOTTISH CASTLE

Trick or treat? Visitors disguised as ghosts, witches, and monsters crowd the old McDuck Castle to celebrate Halloween together. Be careful! Real ghosts, witches, and monsters are hiding among the crowd! Can you spot Huey, Dewey, and Louie in costume? Which of their family members got scared and took refuge in a barrel?

# QUEEN REGINELLA'S PLANET

Donald has traveled through space and time to land on Pacificus. The planet's inhabitants have all gathered to welcome their terrestrial friend. Even Mickey Mouse's friend visiting from the future is here to celebrate the event! Can you spot him?

# BULLET VALLEY

Giddy up! Loyal cowboys are mixed with cattle thieves in the dusty Wild West. Someone wants to snatch the livestock! Spot Sheriff Donald among the gunslingers and the cows as he tries to find the outlaws and lock them up. Which renowned character is here to help, spinning his lasso?

# DUCKBURG STADIUM

The local soccer team has won the final game! The Duckburg fans storm the field to celebrate their beloved champions. Do you see Donald triumphantly raising the Calisota Cup? Which of his friends is still showing off her game-winning soccer skills?

# A MEDIEVAL CITY

Donald and his family have traveled to the past to meet the Duck Family ancestors. Uh-oh, the Beagle Boys have followed them back to medieval Florence! Can you help Donald catch these outlaws before they steal Scrooge's money? Who is playing a sweet melody with a stringed instrument?

# THE BEACH

The Duck Family is enjoying their holiday break!
There's no better place to relax than a sunlit beach.
Can you find a lazy Donald taking a nap? Which of
his relatives are building a lovely sandcastle?

# GYRO'S WORKSHOP

The brilliant inventor has accidentally shrunk all of Duckburg's citizens with one of his inventions! While Little Helper tries to calm the miniaturized crowd, Gyro scrambles to restore his fellow citizens to their original sizes. Donald is unhappy about being shrunk to the size of an ant, as you can see! Which one of Donald's cousins is happy with what he found on Gyro's work table?

# MORE CHARACTERS TO SEARCH AND FIND:

## DUCKBURG

- 🏠 Huey, Dewey, and Louie
- 🏠 Daisy Duck
- 🏠 Scrooge McDuck
- 🏠 Gladstone Gander
- 🏠 Gyro Gearloose
- 🏠 Ludwig Von Drake
- 🏠 Chip 'n' Dale

## GRANDMA DUCK'S FARM

- 🌼 Grandma Duck
- 🌼 Gus Goose
- 🌼 Billy Goat
- 🌼 Scrooge McDuck
- 🌼 Daisy Duck
- 🌼 Huey, Dewey, and Louie

## BEAR MOUNTAIN

- ❄️ Scrooge McDuck
- ❄️ Huey, Dewey, and Louie
- ❄️ Daisy Duck
- ❄️ Gladstone Gander
- ❄️ Ludwig Von Drake

## A SCOTTISH CASTLE

- 🏰 Scrooge McDuck
- 🏰 Huey, Dewey, and Louie
- 🏰 Witch Hazel
- 🏰 Magica De Spell
- 🏰 Ludwig Von Drake

## UNCLE SCROOGE'S MONEY BIN

- 💵 Scrooge McDuck
- 💵 The Beagle Boys
- 💵 Gyro Gearloose
- 💵 Magica De Spell
- 💵 Huey, Dewey, and Louie
- 💵 Pig Mayor

## DUCK AVENGER'S DEN

- 👀 Gyro Gearloose
- 👀 Super Goof
- 👀 The Phantom Blot
- 👀 Emil Eagle
- 👀 Super Daisy
- 👀 Paper Bat
- 👀 Clover Leaf
- 👀 Red Wasp
- 👀 Zafire

## VIKINGS WORLD

- 🔨 Huey, Dewey, and Louie
- 🔨 Scrooge McDuck
- 🔨 Daisy Duck
- 🔨 Gladstone Gander
- 🔨 Gyro Gearloose
- 🔨 Grandma Duck
- 🔨 Pluto

## QUEEN REGINELLA'S PLANET

- 🚀 Huey, Dewey, and Louie
- 🚀 Scrooge McDuck
- 🚀 Gyro Gearloose
- 🚀 Eega Beeva

## BULLET VALLEY

- Huey, Dewey, and Louie
- Daisy Duck
- Minnie Mouse
- Peg-leg Pete
- Mickey Mouse
- Goofy

## A MEDIEVAL CITY

- Scrooge McDuck
- Gyro Gearloose
- The Beagle Boys
- Peg-leg Pete
- Daisy Duck
- Mickey Mouse
- Goofy

## THE BEACH

- Fethry Duck
- José Carioca
- Huey, Dewey, and Louie
- Panchito Pistoles
- Gyro Gearloose
- Magica De Spell

## GYRO'S WORKSHOP

- Scrooge McDuck
- Huey, Dewey, and Louie
- Daisy Duck
- Gladstone Gander
- Fethry Duck
- Ludwig Von Drake
- The Beagle Boys
- Pig Mayor
- Brigitta MacBridge
- Miss Quackfaster
- John D. Rockerduck
- Dickie Duck
- Clara Cluck
- Bertie McGoose

## DUCKBURG STADIUM

- Gyro Gearloose
- Gladstone Gander
- Fethry Duck
- Scrooge McDuck
- Gus Goose
- The Beagle Boys
- José Carioca
- Panchito Pistoles
- Mickey Mouse
- Goofy
- Horace Horsecollar
- Chief O'Hara
- Detective Casey
- Peg-leg Pete
- Portis
- The Phantom Blot
- Eega Beeva
- Doctor Einmug
- Mortimer Mouse
- Daisy Duck
- Huey, Dewey, and Louie
- Minnie Mouse
- Clarabelle Cow
- Grandma Duck

# ANSWERS

**DUCKBURG**

**UNCLE
SCROOGE'S
MONEY
BIN**

# GRANDMA DUCK'S FARM

# DUCK AVENGER'S DEN

# BEAR MOUNTAIN

# VIKINGS WORLD

# A SCOTTISH CASTLE

## QUEEN REGINELLA'S PLANET

## BULLET VALLEY

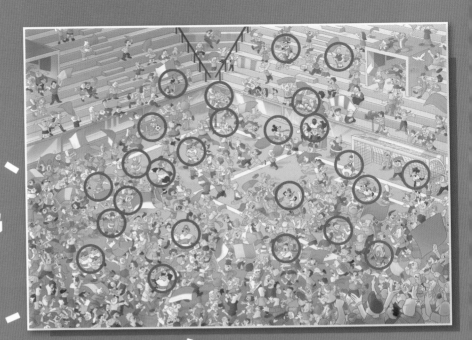

## DUCKBURG STADIUM

## A MEDIEVAL CITY

THE
BEACH

GYRO'S
WORKSHOP